# SOLLY'S not so great ADVENTURE

Written by **Patty Mund**

Illustrated by **Dawn Benson**

Proceeds from the sale of this book will be donated to Strong Tower Ranch in Foristell,
Missouri, to help support its ministry to children and their families. Strong Tower Ranch features
horsemanship and day camps with the goal of providing quality, Christ-centered programs that are
entertaining, character building, and rehabilitating. "Strong Tower" reminds us that we have a
mighty fortress in Christ. We want children, teens and adults who come here to find love and
refuge from a harsh world. Our priority is to help those who are at risk or less fortunate. We are
non-denominational, non-profit and dependent on prayers, financial support and volunteer help.
To find out how you can participate in this ministry, visit us at www.StrongTowerRanch.org.

Special thanks to Vanessa Bays of ByTheButterfly.com for permission to use her font in this book.

To those of us who don't like the idea of being "fenced in" --
God's greatest blessings will come when we embrace the boundaries.

"Trust in the LORD and do good; dwell in the land and enjoy safe pasture.
Take delight in the LORD and He will give you the desires of your heart."
Psalm 37:3-4

On a beautiful ranch
not too far away
a wee foal was born
on a warm summer's day.

As soon as he found his feet he began
to discover the SIGHTS, SMELLS and SOUNDS of the land.

The bluebird's refrain drifting down from the sky,
the whispering wings of the fair butterfly.

The clean smell of rain as it rides on a breeze,
then drips then DROPS on the leaves of the trees.

Each day brought
new wonders,
in fact, even MORE
than all of the
WONDER-filled
days gone before.

But the best thing of all
at the end of each day
was a warm
cozy stall
and a bed of
fresh hay.

And Solomon sang,
"I'm thankful for all
of these beautiful things -
for bird songs and raindrops and butterfly wings.
WERE ALL OF THESE WONDERS MADE SPECIAL FOR ME?
This place is the best! It's where I want to be."

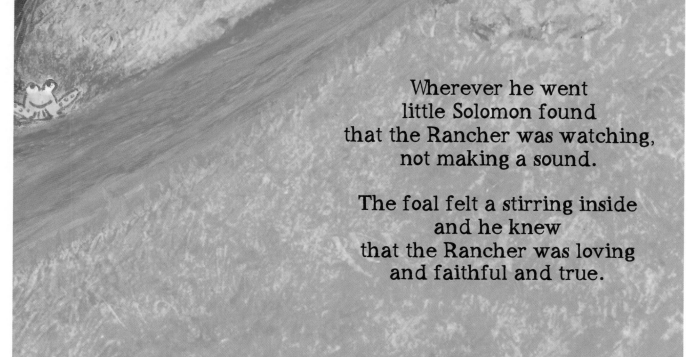

Wherever he went
little Solomon found
that the Rancher was watching,
not making a sound.

The foal felt a stirring inside
and he knew
that the Rancher was loving
and faithful and true.

When Solly felt hungry the Rancher would lead
him to the best pasture grown from the best seed.

Nearby was a stream, so refreshing and cool,
and they'd stop there to drink from the still, sparkling pool.

When Solly was hurt or came down with the flu,
the kind Rancher always knew just what to do.

If thunder clouds came and created a storm,
the Rancher made sure Solly stayed dry and warm.

As each day of wonder came to an end,
the foal drifted off, dreaming of his dear friend.

Solomon wanted to learn and explore
so he asked lots of questions and then asked some more.

The Rancher spoke softly, yet Solomon heard,
for he paid close attention to every word.

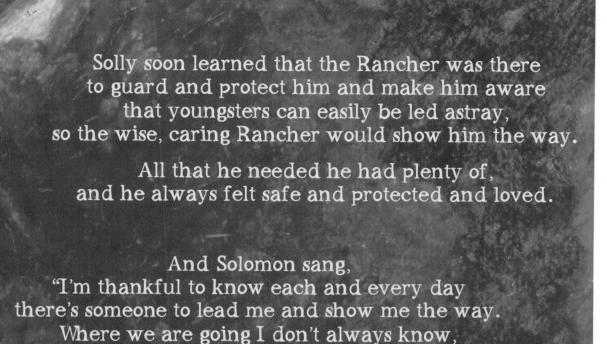

Solly soon learned that the Rancher was there
to guard and protect him and make him aware
that youngsters can easily be led astray,
so the wise, caring Rancher would show him the way.

All that he needed he had plenty of,
and he always felt safe and protected and loved.


And Solomon sang,
"I'm thankful to know each and every day
there's someone to lead me and show me the way.
Where we are going I don't always know,
but I'll follow the Rancher wherever he goes.."

Little Solomon grew and in no time at all
it was hard to believe he had ever been small.

As his head got too big and his legs made him taller,
he started to think that the ranch looked much smaller.

He thought of himself much more than he should
and was no longer thankful for all that was good.
The things that to him once seemed wondrous and rare,
he no longer noticed - or no longer cared.

The kind Rancher Solomon used to adore
wanted Solly to follow him, just like before.

But Solomon paid no attention, for he
was too busy thinking, "IT'S ALL ABOUT ME".

And Solomon grumbled,
"My life's not exciting; I deserve **SO** much more.
I want to go places I've not been before.
I suppose that old Rancher thinks I ought to stay,
but out on my own - I would do things **MY** way!"

Then he noticed a gate that was opened a crack,
and he walked right on through it and didn't look back.

He ran fast and far and exclaimed, "Look at me!"
"No boundaries, no fences, at last I am free!"

He galloped UP one hill and rolled DOWN another.
He jumped over one rock and then every other.

He'd had quite a day and was feeling alright...

...'til a thunderstorm made for a dark, **SCARY** night.

He stumbled and fumbled without really knowing
which way was the best way for him to be going.
He was wet, cold and weary, and to his dismay,
there was no cozy stall - no bed of fresh hay.

And Solomon moaned,
"I'm tired and I'm cold and I want to be fed!
I wish I could sleep in my warm, cozy bed."
He shivered all night, afraid and awake,
too proud to admit that he'd made a mistake.

All through the night his poor tummy grumbled,
yet even then Solomon still wasn't humbled.

"There's a field of green grass
that will fill up my tummy!"
But the foul, bitter weeds
were not at all yummy.

Solomon desperately
needed a drink -
his mind quickly changed
when he noticed the stink.

He discovered a tree and exclaimed, "What a treat!"
The shiny red fruit was especially sweet.
There was no need to stop at an apple or two,
since no one was there telling him what to do.

So he ate and he ate, and kept eating until
he couldn't stand up - he'd had more than his fill!

And Solomon whined,
"The grass and the water that looked so delicious
were rather disgusting, and far from nutritious.
I'm tired and I'm thirsty - does anyone care?!
Oh, why am I suffering?  Life just isn't fair!"

He was losing all hope as he wandered around,
searching for things that could never be found
away from his home and the friend he'd neglected
who'd faithfully nurtured and loved and protected.

He began to remember and started to dream
of the lovely green pasture and cool, sparkling stream,
the SIGHTS, SMELLS and SOUNDS - all the wonderful things -
the bluebird's sweet song and the butterfly's wings.

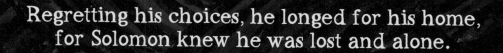

Regretting his choices, he longed for his home,
for Solomon knew he was lost and alone.

It caused him GREAT sorrow to think that his folly
brought heartache to one who'd done so much for Solly.

And Solomon cried,
"I thought if I did what was pleasing to me,
my life would be better and I would be free.
I foolishly wanted to be on my own,
but I'm lonely and sad and I want to go home!"

Solly would learn he had no need to fear,
for his dear friend, the Rancher, had always been near.
As much as he'd wanted the horse to return,
the Rancher knew Solly had lessons to learn.

So the Rancher had patiently left him alone
until Solly was ready to follow him home.

At first Solly thought
that his eyes had deceived him,
but the Rancher had actually
come to RETRIEVE him!

Consoled and relieved
that it wasn't too late,
he followed the Rancher
back home through the gate...

He left the gate open, and Solly asked why.
With wisdom and love, the Rancher replied,

"Taking away your
freedom to choose
would keep you from growing
and learning the truth.
It's a choice you must make
each and every day
to stay here with me
or to go your own way."

"In life there are boundaries that help you to know
the right path to take - the best way to go.
Without them you'd wander around, as you've learned,
lost and confused about which way to turn."


And Solomon sang,
"Thank you for being my good, faithful friend!
You patiently waited for me even when
I wandered away, though I knew all along,
that wherever **YOU** are is where I belong."

Then suddenly Solomon realized that he had learned what it means to **truly** be free. Having the freedom to do what he **could** did not necessarily mean that he **should**.

There's freedom in choosing to do the right thing,
embracing the BLESSINGS that boundaries bring.

## Psalm 19:7-11

The law of the LORD is perfect,
    refreshing the soul.
The statutes of the LORD are trustworthy,
    making wise the simple.
The precepts of the LORD are right,
    giving joy to the heart.
The commands of the LORD are radiant,
    giving light to the eyes.
The fear of the LORD is pure,
    enduring forever.
The decrees of the LORD are firm,
    and all of them are righteous.
They are more precious than gold,
    than much pure gold;
they are sweeter than honey,
    than honey from the honeycomb.
By them your servant is warned;
    in keeping them there is great reward.

# God's Special Plan for You!

God made the world and everything in it, including you! He loves you and wants to be your friend. But there is a BIG problem.

God is holy – He never does anything wrong or bad, and because He is holy, He hates sin. Sin is anything we think, say or do that is not pleasing to God. And the Bible says that EVERYONE sins. This is the problem – we can't be friends with God, until we get rid of our sin. But there is nothing WE can do about our sin. We might try very hard, but we will still sin sometimes.

God made a way to solve our sin problem. God's son, Jesus, came to earth as a baby, lived a perfect life, but then He was punished for the sins of everyone in the world. He was killed by angry people who hated Him, but He loved them enough to die for their sins and ours. Three days later Jesus came back to life! God is more powerful than death and sin!

God's friendship is a gift for us that we did not do anything to earn. We call this "grace". It's just like a birthday present – we don't have to work for it. All we have to do is take it from the giver.

2 Corinthians 5:21 says, "For He made Him (Jesus) who knew no sin to be sin for us, that we might become the righteousness of God in Him."

This Bible verse means that when we accept God's gift of grace, He doesn't see our sin any more. He sees us the same way He sees His Son – perfect and without sin. This doesn't mean that we stop sinning or we become perfect. It means that God forgives our sins when we tell Him we are sorry and ask Him to forgive us.

When you accept God's free gift of grace, you become His friend and His child, and He also gives you other gifts – eternal life in Heaven with Him, and His Holy Spirit who helps you live for Him while you're here on the earth!

Romans 10:9-10 says, "That if you confess with your mouth, 'Jesus is Lord,' and believe in your heart that God raised him from the dead, you will be saved. For it is with your heart that you believe and are justified, and it is with your mouth that you confess and are saved."

God wants to be your Savior and your Lord. This means that he wants you to give your life to Him completely, and let Him be the boss! He wants you to get to know Him better. You can grow in your relationship with God by telling Him you're sorry when you sin, talking to Him every day, reading and obeying the Bible, telling others about Him, and going to church and Sunday School.

"Trust in the LORD
and do good; dwell in
the land and enjoy
safe pasture.
Take delight in the LORD
and He will give you the
desires of your heart."
Psalm 37:3-4

Made in the USA
Charleston, SC
02 December 2013